This book is dedicated to our children.

**union
square
kids**

NEW YORK

UNION SQUARE KIDS and the distinctive Union Square Kids logo are trademarks of Union Square & Co., LLC.

Union Square & Co., LLC, is a subsidiary of Sterling Publishing Co., Inc.

ISBN 978-1-4549-4544-4

Library of Congress Cataloging-in-Publication Data

Names: Mrs. & Mr. MacLeod, author, illustrator.
Title: How to eat a book / Mrs. & Mr. MacLeod.
Description: New York : Union Square Kids, [2022] | Audience: Ages 3 to 8.
 | Audience: Grades K-1. | Summary: One by one, Sheila, Gerald and
 Geraldine are eaten by books, throwing them into strange lands where
 Sheila escapes the weight of the world entirely, Gerald braves the
 wonder of seeing it up close, and Geraldine turns as terrifically
 terrible as she possibly can.
Identifiers: LCCN 2021061854 | ISBN 9781454945444 (hardcover)
Subjects: CYAC: Books and reading--Fiction. | LCGFT: Picture books.
Classification: LCC PZ7.1.M4263 Ho 2022 | DDC [E]--dc23
LC record available at https://lccn.loc.gov/2021061854

For information about custom editions, special sales, and premium purchases,
please contact specialsales@unionsqareandco.com.

Printed in China

Lot #:
2 4 6 8 10 9 7 5 3 1

07/22

unionsquareandco.com

Cover and interior art and design by Mrs. & Mr. MacLeod

HOW to EAT A BOOK

MRS. & MR. MACLEOD

union
square
kids

NEW YORK

Sheila sat down to eat her first book,

and the *strangest thing happened* . . .

The book ate HER.

Sheila's cousin Gerald
sensed something *stranger* still.

His left foot
went left.

His right foot
went *wrong*.

And then . . .

The book ate HIM.

Gerald's twin sister,
Geraldine,
watched it all

and *sipped her tea*.

And the tea grew *tired* of Geraldine.

And Geraldine
grew *tired* of tea!

So . . .

She grabbed the BIGGEST book
she could find *AND* . . .

The book did
NOT eat Geraldine.

(Until it did.)

Devoured by their books,

Sheila, Gerald, and Geraldine
could no longer hear the
"Coo-coo!"
of Grandma's
ticktock clock.

Spiraling into a world of words,

Hungry for answers,

Sheila asked
a *beautiful* question.

$$Z_n + 1 = Z_n^2 + c$$

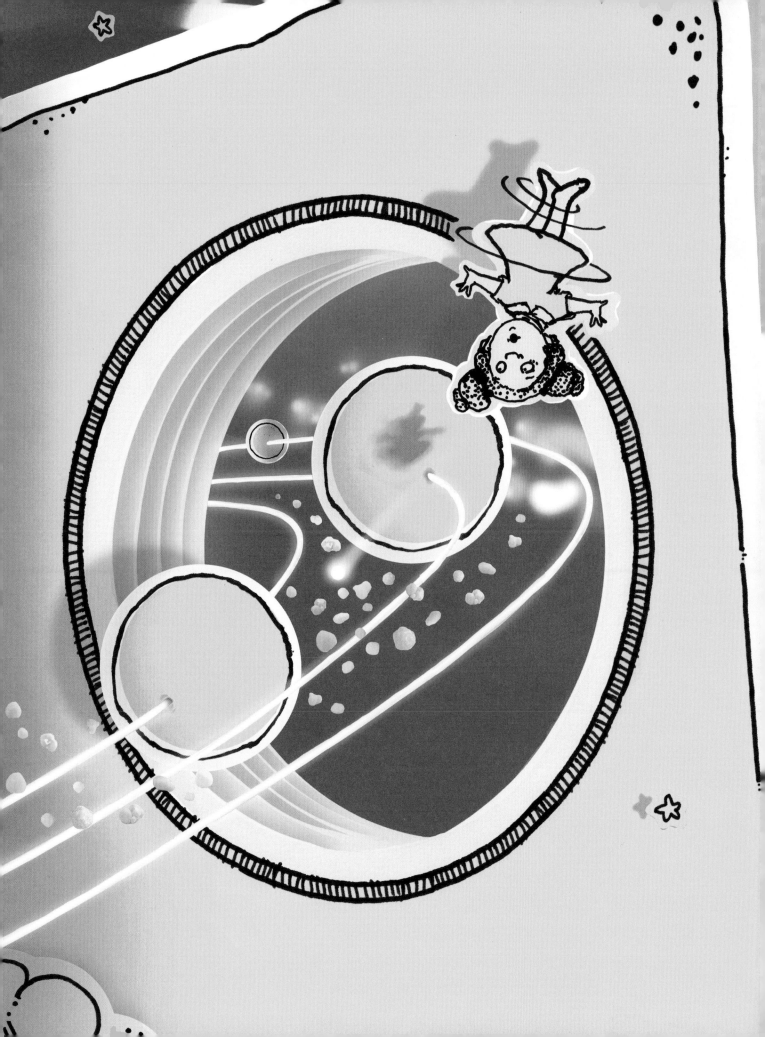

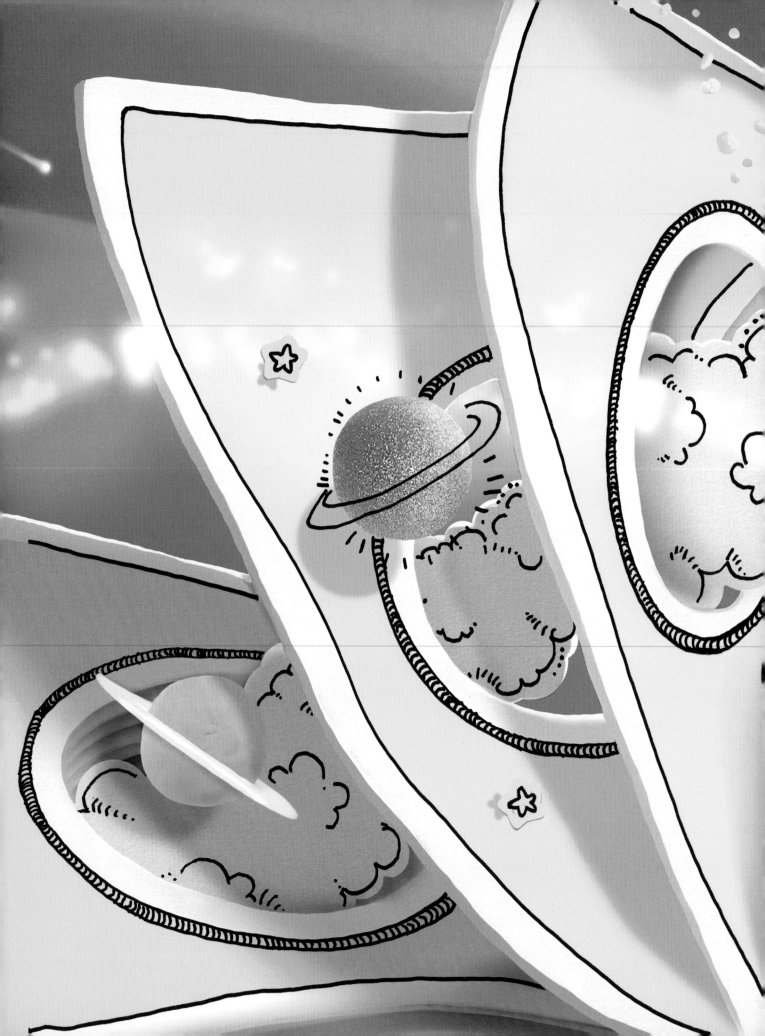

In *search*,
Sheila BLASTED OFF!

Through giants made of *gas*.

Past planets made of *diamonds*.

Into a Space—

Where what goes up, doesn't always come down.

Hiding between
the lines of his book,
the sounds of the *Bug-a-Boo* called out.

G

E R A L D

Gerald followed the letters into the Ever—

—that Never had been.

Gerald found the Bug-a-Boo
and the Bug-a-Boo found *him*.

Unleashed by her book,

Geraldine BURST FREE
from her wall-to-wall
carpeted cage.

Geraldine tore through the pages,
to a time where being *terrible* was terrific.

And Geraldine
was *terrific* at being terrible.

And the *Books*
began
to realize

SOMETHING
STRANGE

was happening.

But it was *too late*.

The children were

EAT
THE
BO

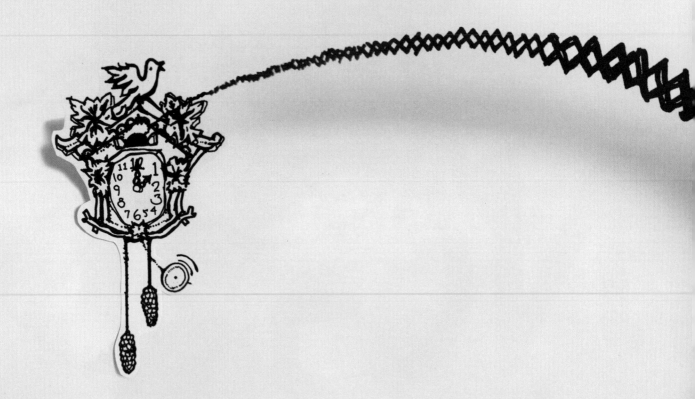

Until, there were no words left.

Strangely,
something remained.

Sheila's How?
Discovered a *Why*,
and opened up

a *What if* ?

Gerald liked being lost,
and *loved* being found.

And Geraldine

would *never* be tamed.

Strange it is,

strange but true,

the way to eat a book,

is to *let*